MW01140397

In Jesus Name & For His Glory

Jim Galbraith

There is Something About an Aqua Velva Man

Read this book and find out what it is!

Kim Z. read 7/09

by

James C Galbraith

authorHOUSE®

AuthorHouse™
1663 Liberty Drive, Suite 200
Bloomington, IN 47403
www.authorhouse.com
Phone: 1-800-839-8640

First published by AuthorHouse   12/23/2008

ISBN: 978-1-4343-4712-1 (hc)
ISBN: 978-1-4343-4711-4 (sc)

Library of Congress Control Number: 2008900071

Printed in the United States of America
Bloomington, Indiana

This book is printed on acid-free paper.

BIOGRAPHY

JAMES CONOVER GALBRAITH

Jim was born in 1926 in Philadelphia, PA. He served in the U.S. Coast Guard during World War II as a sonar operator aboard a U.S. Navy frigate, escorting convoys from Boston to North Africa.

He had an amazing life as a TV actor for commercial ads, including the popular after-shave lotion, AQUA VELVA with actress Mamie Van Doren and many other commercials; plus a distinguished business career with Amway Company.

A significant event in his later life was a decision to run for a Republican seat in Congress in Washington State. Although he lost this race, it led to the beginning of his political organization,

FACTS FOR FREEDOM, a conservative Christian group, of which he is the Founder and President.

FACTS publishes a monthly *ACTION*GRAM newsletter, informing readers what is happening in Congress, the courts, and the media, about the anti-Christ, anti-Jesus, anti-Bible, and anti-Christian crowd; with suggestions of what faithful Christians can do to combat the attacks of these enemies in this spiritual war.

Jim also publishes a voters' guide for every election, based on the candidates he feels Christians would want to vote for.

Jim is an avid fisherman, and loves to garden and to read. He was married for 60 years, and in January 2006 his precious wife left him to be with the Lord. His oldest son Jim Jr. died from a blood clot in his lungs when he was only 52 years old. He has one daughter and one other son, nine grandchildren and four great- grandchildren. ALL know the Lord, and there has never been a divorce in his family. Four family members are married, and their spouses all have been saved. In addition, Jim has led hundreds of people in many places to accept Jesus Christ as their Savior.

ACKNOWLEDGEMENTS

to those who played a big part in inspiring me
and encouraging me to write this book.

Also gratitude goes to those
who held me up in prayer,

and for the Holy Spirit's guidance,
wisdom and prayer;

Our son Keith and our daughter Helen
and their families;

Lauri Schiffman

Chuck Murray

Robby Tuthill

Bryce and Emily Wegner

Pastor John Nocera

and Alice Jackson, who typed,
edited and printed many
drafts and placed photographs where needed,
and without whom this book
would never have been organized and started.

PRESENT AFFILIATIONS

FACTS FOR FREEDOM -- Founder and President for 28 years

Monthly Newsletter; Monthly Rallies ;

FACTS Endorsement Sheet for Every Election

Speaking at Rallies, Church Services, Youth Retreats,
and other meetings

MINISTRY -- Bread of Life Homeless Mission, Seattle;

Board of Directors; Speaking Monthly

FORMER

Appearance on TV with 700 Club

AMWAY Business Leader

Candidate for Congressman of Washington State

Previous President of Young Men's Republican Club

Keynote Leader at Weekend Retreats

Youth Groups -- Sunday School Teacher

ENDORSERS

BOB WILLIAMS
Founder and President, Evergreen Freedom Foundation

ROB MCKENNA
Washington State Attorney General

VAL STEVENS
Washington State Senator

RICH DE VOSS
President and Founder, AMWAY Corporation

PASTOR JOE FEUTIN
Founder, WERG (Washington State Evangelicals for
a Righteous Government)

RICK FORCIER
President, Christian Coalition of Washington State

DON MCALVENY
President and Founder, International Collectors' Association

CHARLES NAM, M.D.
My Personal Physician

ENDORSEMENTS

"Jim Galbraith has been an inspiration to me since 1984 with his persistent drive to ensure our freedoms are preserved. Jim has been a leader in sounding the alarm that the enemy 'has saturated every facet of our courts, government, schools and culture' through his FACTS network.

"Jim's book describes what happens when the life of a sinner is turned over to God. Jim gives credit for his families' abundant life to Mathew 6:33, 'Seek you first the Kingdom of God and all these things (the abundant life) will be added unto you.'

"This book is an encouragement for all of us because it shows what happens when someone puts Christ first and allows the Lord to work through them.

"Jim's bottom line is 'are you assured of where you will spend eternity?' If not, now is the time to accept Christ."

★ **Bob Williams, President**
Evergreen Freedom Foundation

"Dear Jim,

"Blessings to you in the New Year and may your strength and willingness to serve continue throughout.

"This is my 'words of wisdom' as they came to me while considering your autobiography.

"Jim is one of a kind! His life is an inspiration to all who know and love him. He continues to encourage me today as he has for the many years I have known him."

★ **Senator Val Stevens [Washington State]**

Dear Mr. Galbraith:

"It was very nice to speak with you over the phone today. I wish you much success with your book. Below you will find the text of Rob McKenna's message that you requested for the cover of the book:

"In this moving testimony to the power and value of faith, Jim Galbraith reminds us all to <u>live</u> the example that we preach."

★ **Rob McKenna, Attorney General, Washington State**

"I have known Jim since 2001. He is a sincere, dedicated Christian whose honor and integrity is above reproach. To read his book is to glean just a small portion of this man who is a blessing to all who know him."

★ **Dr. John Nocera, Pastor** Summit Christian Center
   Tacoma, WA

"From Aqua Velva man to making advertisements in Europe to starting a successful business, Jim Galbraith kept making his dreams come true. Through it all, he gave all credit and glory to God for his fascinating life. This is a success story with a lot of heart."

★ **Rich DeVos**, President, Amway Corp. (Quixtar)

DEDICATION

This Book is dedicated to Hilda,
my precious wife of
60 years.
What an influence she had on me, our children,
friends, and hundreds of others
who knew her.
Proverbs 31:25 -- "She is a woman of strength
and dignity and has no fear of old age.
"When she speaks, her words are wise, and kindness
is the rule for everything she says."

And that was my Hildy !

FOREWORD

This book is about a man's exciting pilgrimage in a life of power, influence and victory as an authentic follower of Jesus Christ. It is a story that will stir you with motivation and inspiration to experience the incredible, real presence of Christ to guide and provide according to His promise of "life and life abundant". It truly chronicles an astonishing fulfillment that can happen to anyone who will make the decision Jim Galbraith made.

In light of my close friendship with Jim and his family over four decades, I have the privilege now of inviting you into the story of his life as it challenges and proves that a personal relationship with God has awesome surprises and benefits.

My first experience with Jim came when as a new seminary graduate I began my pastoral ministry in the Prebyterian church in Salem, New Jersey. One day a handsome, vigorous young man and his beautiful wife and children came on the scene. He was a religious skeptic to say the least, who was rapidly charging to the heights of success and fame in New York City as a male model and actor when something happened in his life to abruptly change his character and goals. This book is really about the transforming 'Person' he met and the positive powerful impact that 'Person' has had on Jim, his family, and countless numbers of people over many years. This fast moving, honest autobiography is truly engaging.

One of the most inspiring touches Jim had on my ministry was when he became the point person in what was recognized as a genuine revival in the town of Salem, New Jersey. Subsequently, Jim was personally interviewed by David Brinkley as part of an NBC national telecast focusing on uniquely significant facts about the town of Salem. As Jim's pastor, this evidence of what God can do with a sincerely dedicated young man gave me a life long and personally confirming witness to the positive power of a man filled with the Holy Spirit.

Over the years we have been taken in different directions and places but we have always connected from time to time because I treasured our friendship and I was abundantly nourished in my faith by any contact I would have with Him and his family. What you will read in this book includes many of the wonderful and exciting activities and events in an ongoing saga of consistent faith and courageous acts. This is a story that grips the heart with hunger for God's way.

I am excited for you as I commend this fascinating story of Jim Galbraith's journey, and most especially as he points you to the real subject of this book, Jesus Christ.

Thank you Jim for the enormous part you played as an "exhibit A" confirmation of the belief I have lived and proclaimed over half a century.

Rev. Charles K. Murray Jr. H.R.
Presbyterian Church USA

OUTLINE

- ★ Opening story: Before Christ
- ★ Jim's early life; his parents; joining the Coast Guard
- ★ Military service, 1944- 1945
- ★ Jim and Hilda meet and marry , 1945
  Children , work , timcs and places
- ★ Building home in New Jersey
  Moving to new home.
- ★ Changing work location
  New job, work for Philadelphia newspaper
- ★ Challenges to life and marriage
- ★ Influence of Chuck Murray
- ★ Finding Christ, new life based on faith
- ★ Career in advertising , in U.S. and in Europe
  Travels to different countries
- ★ Return to U.S. and advertising career
- ★ Children's lives as they grew older.
- ★ Starting Amway business
  Travels, meetings, other Amway connections
- ★ Vacation in Canada, decision to move to Belleville
- ★ Amway business, life there, church and friends in Canada
- ★ Jim's articles in Guidepost magazine
- ★ Decision to move to Kenmore, near Seattle

Buying a home in Kenmore, family, friends, Amway business, meetings

★ Jim deciding to run for Congress in 1984, losing election

★ Starting FACTS FOR FREEDOM organization

Beliefs and views, statements and newsletter, election endorsements

★ Jim's boyhood life and how that compares to today's morals

★ Selling Kenmore home, moving to Kingston

Organizations: Young Men's Republican Club

Bread of Life homeless ministry

★ Moving to Puyallup, new church

★ James' life and story

★ Other children, their lives and developing careers and achievements

Grandchildren and extended family

★ About Hilda

★ Writing this book, "There's Something About an Aqua-Velva Man………."

★ The Gift

★ Jim's life today and tomorrow

PHOTOS IN BOOK

1 -- Cover, Jim, Aqua Velva Man
2 -- Jim, Biography page
3 -- Hilda and baby, Dedication page
4 -- Hilda in uniform
5 -- Jim in uniform, sitting on steps
6 -- Jim's & Hilda's wedding
7 -- Bill & Jim in uniforms
8 -- Hilda skiing
9 -- Hilda & Jim in choir gowns
10 - Old brick farmhouse
11 - New white house
12 - Jim with cast on leg
13 - Jim with Mamie Van Doren
14 - Jim sitting in chair with two children
15 - 18 - Jim in 4 small photos using telephones
19 - White farm home, with addition
20 - Van, tent, with daughter Helen
21 - Hilda & Helen; scenic fountain & buildings
22 - People on street corner
23 - Helen & Hilda in archway
24 - Jim with 2 children; M&M commercial
25 - Jim, ad -- water skiing
26 - Jim with Carol Burnett
27 - Chuck & Nancy Murray by fireplace
28 -- Nancy Murray with Amway products
29 - Large cruise ship
30 -- Smaller yacht
31 -- Rich De Vos (dark hair)

32 -- Jay van Andel (light hair)

33 -- Rob Roy, wife & daughters (one in cap & gown)

34 -- Hank & Margaret Demark

35 -- Large cabin

36-38 - Small log cabin

39 -- Bill & Verda Linn, on patio

40 -- Jim & Hilda in boat

41 - Trees in snow

42 -- Son James by snow machine

43 - Large Kenmore home

44 - Pounds family, sitting on bench

45 - son Keith, with Leah and 3 daughters

46 -- Jim &Family, with Hilda sitting in front

47 - Hilda with son James

48 - Jim & Hilda, children on horses

49 - Dick & Dee Ossinger

50 -- Jim, Galbraith for Congress

51 -- Jim & Hilda w/Pastor & wife

52 -- Horses

53 - Galbraith family wedding

54 - Jim & Dave with Infiniti

55 - Jim & Gen Graham

56 - President Reagan

57 - Jim & brother Bob as boys

58 -- Jim - "WE WIN !! "

INTRODUCTION

This book is the story of the 82 years I have spent on this Earth. The reason and purpose for writing this is for you to read and draw a comparison to my life when I just lived for me the world, the flesh and the devil, and all the sin, trash and emptiness they produced; then to see the exciting changes in me and my family when we surrendered our lives to Jesus Christ and followed Him, the Way, the Truth and the Life; most of all, the abundant life it produced as Jesus promised, if we just follow Him!

Forty-five years ago my life was a first-class mess. I hated myself, couldn't stand being around my wife Hilda and our three kids and resented having to take care of them. I was going down a one-way street leading nowhere. Cheating, stealing and lying were a way of life for me.

Little by little, I became mean and got drunk every night and started to cheat on Hilda. I lied and committed adultery every chance I could. I never hit Hilda but I sure abused her verbally. At that time I cared less about what effect that had on her and our children. I treated her so badly that she wound up in the hospital with ulcers.

While she was in the Salem, NJ hospital, Chuck Murray, a young pastor from the Salem Presbyterian Church introduced her to Jesus Christ. All her fears, anxieties and anger left her, and she became filled with joy and peace. When I brought her home, she wasn't the same woman I had taken to the hospital. Something dramatic had happened to her. After awhile, I wanted what she had.

One evening in June 1961 I had invited Chuck and Nancy Murray to our house for dinner. Afterwards Chuck prayed with me to confess that I was a sinner, ask for forgiveness, and ask Jesus to take over my life.

When I did that all the sin, filth and corruption of my past was forgiven and forgotten by God. I John 1:19 -- "If we confess our sins He is faithful and just to forgive us our sins and cleanse us from all unrighteousness."

Here are some of the blessings and abundant life Hilda, the kids and I have had for 45 years.

As it is written: I Cor 2;9 -- "No eye has seen , no ear has heard, no mind has conceived what God has prepared for those who love Him (L.B.)

Psalm 37: 4-5 -- "Be delighted with the Lord. Then He will give you all your heart's desires. Commit everything you do to the Lord. Trust Him to help you and He will."

CHAPTER ONE

When I was a little boy growing up, America was going through the Great Depression of the 1930s. My father and grandfather owned the Galbraith Paving Company; they had a lot of customers who owed them large amounts of money, but were unable to pay their bills for work done.

As a result the business went bankrupt, and my father gave up. He began to drink a lot and became very depressed. One day he shut himself up in the garage, turned on the car engine, and sat there until he died.

I was 5 or 6 years old and was there when family members found him and pulled him from the car; I remember them putting a mirror by his nose to see if he was still breathing, but it was too late.

At that time my mother had to work to support me and my brother Bob, and was unable to take care of us. Her friend got us into the Hershey Industrial School in Hershey, PA. Bob stayed there and graduated from high school, then went to school to study electrical engineering.

My mother married Wes Weber, a supervisor at the Minneapolis Honeywell Instrument Company. I came home from Hershey and lived with them in Philadelphia. From the start, Wes Weber resented me and made my life miserable. Eventually my mother divorced him, and that was the first divorce ever in my family.

In high school I was a very poor student who majored in girls and football. After World War II broke out, I quit school in the 10th grade and joined the U.S. Coast Guard at age 16. I lied about my age, you had to be 17. All my friends from high school and older friends had already enlisted, and I wanted to get into the war like they did. I was supposed to go to boot camp in Manhattan Beach, NY, but there was a measles epidemic there, so I couldn't go for six weeks -- my friends had given me a goodbye party and there I still was, it was embarrassing, hilarious too -I had to hide all the time.

The Coast Guard sent me to the Coast Guard Academy in New London, Connecticut, where they trained me to be a sonar operator. I was then shipped to the US Navy frigate USS Key West, where I spent two years protecting the convoys from Boston to North Africa.

Hilda Slaughter was the first woman Chief Radio Operator in the Coast Guard. I met her at the USO Buddy's Club in Boston. She was a knockout in her uniform, and I was a salty sailor who thought he knew it all at 17. She was standing at the edge of the dance floor, watching people dance. I walked over (Mr. Big Shot) and asked her sarcastically, "How long have you been in the service?" With a sweet smile she said, "Three years. How long have you been in?" I sure felt like a fool.

Hilda was on her way to stand her 12 midnight to 8 AM watch at the top of the Customs Building, which at the time was the tallest building in Boston. I walked with her to work, and we kinda liked each other and started to date. She had auburn hair and beautiful legs, and a melting smile. What she saw in me I'll never know. We took walks in the Public Gardens, went to movies --and there was a place where we would go and have a couple of beers.

A week later my ship left for North Africa. I remember one night when I was standing watch at 0300, and we were in the middle of the North Atlantic, and had just received a radio warning that a German submarine wolf pack was in our area. I was standing on the bridge looking down at the black water, imagining a torpedo coming right at us. Boy was I scared. I thought, "For this you lied about your age".

When we got back six weeks later, I had our signalman flash a message to the top of the Customs Building: "Hilda Slaughter, meet Jim 8:00 PM at the corner of Beacon and Pine." Now is that romantic, or what?

Just to show you what a hotshot sailor I thought I was who knew it all at 17, one night I was walking through Scully Square in Boston on my way to pick up Hilda after her watch ended.

At the time there was an American Legion convention going on, and an intoxicated celebrant approached me and told me his daughter always wanted a sailor's hat. Would I swap my sailor hat for his American Legion cap? So I did.

I walked about two blocks and was stopped by a Shore Patrolman who told me, "You are out of uniform. Where is your hat?" I said, "I lost it."

He said, "Go and get one." I replied, "Where can I get a sailor hat at midnight?" About that time a civilian cop jumped in and said to me, "Watch the way you talk to this S.P.", and I answered,

"What business is that of yours?" (one of the many dumb things I did during the war). The S.P. immediately arrested me and I was thrown into the brig. I remember a drunken submarine Captain in the cell next to mine, beating his head against the bars. What a night! They let me out at dawn and I immediately went to Hilda's apartment, expecting a lot of sympathy. When she opened the door she looked at me and said, "You big dummy, why didn't you keep your big mouth shut?" One of her coworkers was on her way to work at the time and told Hilda the story. Why she didn't stop seeing me is beyond me.

When the war with Germany ended in May 1945 I was sent to a rest camp at the tip of Cape Cod, MA, awaiting my discharge. Hilda was still on duty in Boston and I couldn't wait to see her. Boston was 165 miles away, and I would hitchhike to Boston just to be with her out on a date, then I would hitchhike back. Man, was I in love.

I told her how much I loved her and wanted her to marry me and we would live in Philadelphia. I was 19 and she was 26, and my brother Bob tried to talk her out of marrying me, that I was too immature, but that didn't matter to her.

I was discharged and we finally got married on Feb 9th, 1946, in Boston. For me that was the best part to come out of WW II. That was 60 years ago -- being married that long is a rarity; today more than 50% of the people who get married later get divorced.

(Later in life our age difference turned out to be a blessing, because when she became really sick I was still strong enough to help her and take care of her.)

Because Hilda was still in the Coast Guard, and the U.S. was still at war with Japan, she had to get permission from her Commanding Officer to be married in a wedding dress. It was a court martial offense during wartime to be caught out of uniform in public.

Hilda was born in Pickens, WV. Her father and brother worked in the coal mines in Pennsylvania. Her brother Bill was a Marine, her brother Paul was a sailor, Hilda and her sister Fran were in the Coast Guard. Fran's husband was in the Army . All four branches of the service were covered by the Slaughter Family.

Hilda and I spent our honeymoon skiing at Franconia, NH. Having little money, we debated if we should buy her an engagement ring or go on a honeymoon ? No ring, but we had a great time on our honeymoon!

We stayed in this small hotel. I always open the window when I go to bed. It gets really cold in NH at night, so guess what happened ? The water pipe froze and

burst and flooded out the cocktail lounge below.-- the owner had just finished remodeling the room.

I used the hotel's kitchen and baked Hilda an apple pie. The owner offered me a job to be their cook. At least he forgave me for the flooded cocktail lounge.

Hilda and I went to live with my Mother in Germantown, Philadelphia, PA. She kept that 3-bedroom house so that after the war her boys would have a home to come back to. Bob was living there as well. She worked in the office of a steel mill and had lived there alone during the war; she also served as an air raid warden and used to go out every night and patrol the neighborhood, and that took courage.

Hilda and I both joined the choir at the Presbyterian Church. After choir practice, we always walked (no car) to the Germantown Tavern and drank beer. We wobbled home, because you shouldn't drink and drive -- no problem if you don't have a car.

When we moved in with Mom, all we had was a few hundred dollars' mustering-out pay, and our uniforms for a wardrobe. But we were young and in love. What really helped was the 52-20 Club from the GI Bill of Rights -- that

was $20 each for 52 weeks. forty dollars a week was a good income then.

I was working at Glenn L. Martin Aircraft Company as a supervisor; we were making spare parts for fighter airplanes. Their contract ran out so I walked across the lot to the Cadillac agency and they hired me as an auto salesman. Hilda and I moved into our own house. Our two sons, James and Keith, were born there in Philadelphia in 1950 and 1952; our daughter Helen was born after we moved to NJ.

Even while I was living with my Mom, I was impatient to start building my own house, on the farm property originally owned by my great-grandfather, Truitt Perry; I had been dreaming about this for years; at this time it belonged to my Uncle Al. My great-grandfather, who lived to be 99, farmed this land, 99 acres. He used to take

his produce to Woodstown with his horse and buggy. The old brick farmhouse was built in 1700. At one time it was a Catholic church run by Jesuit priests, called the Keiger House.

At that time the Catholics in Philadelphia were being persecuted by the British; the Catholics had to get in a boat and go down the Delaware River, then go up Salem Creek to reach the church.

Uncle Al sold me 1.9 acres for $500; he said I could pay him later. (I paid him five years later.) Then my brother Bob, who was an engineer, drew up plans for me after I told him what I wanted.

Finally we got started. On weekends I used to drive to the farm and work until it got dark. Then I would turn on the car headlights and keep on working. I sure was an eager beaver. It's amazing what you can do if you have a dream and a goal and go after it full bore.

I remember the time when a man I had hired was down in the hole he was digging for our well, and our son James, who was 7, was kicking dirt down on him. James thought it was funny but the well-digger didn't. He hollered up that "If you don't get that kid out of there you can get someone else to dig your well !" A good spanking works wonders.

When we had the roof on, the windows and doors installed, the water system and septic tank working, electricity hooked up, and a space heater in place, we moved in.

The builder drove his flatbed truck to our house at West Oak Lane in Philadelphia to get our belongings. We got everything loaded and tied down with a tarp on top. We didn't care if we looked like a bunch of dust-bowl refugees on the move, we were on our way to start a brand-new beginning.

When we arrived we unloaded the truck into a house with a cement floor, wallboard with nails showing and nothing painted inside -- there was a lot of work ahead. We lived there 22 years. Our daughter Helen Applegate was born in Woodbury, NJ in 1959.

The 60-mile commute to the Cadillac agency was too long, so after about a year I got a job at Courtesy Chevrolet in Penns Grove, NJ, only ten minutes from home.

One day while I was working on the roof of the house, the scaffold came loose and I fell about 20 feet and broke my right leg. I was rushed to the hospital where the bone was reset and a cast was put on from the top of my leg down to my foot. I spent 10 days in the hospital, and it was five months before the cast came off. All this time my brother and friends kept working on the house for us.

I had to keep working at Courtesy even with the cast on my leg, as it was the only income I had.

During this time I was also singing with bands in night clubs and at dances. Shortly after the cast was removed, I had a gig singing with a band at a high school senior prom. It was snowing that night, and I was wearing a thin silk tuxedo. On the way

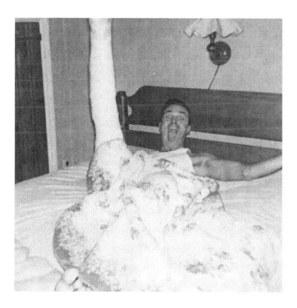

home after the dance, I pulled into the dirt road leading to our house, and it was blocked by a two-foot snowdrift. I opened the car trunk to get my snow shovel and it wasn't there. My boys, 12 and 10 at the time, had taken it to build a snow fort and failed to put it back. Needless to say I was very upset as I had to walk 1 1/2 miles in a blizzard across the uneven fields to get home. By the time I got there I was really angry, but I waited until morning when I had calmed down to give the boys a very strong lecture on the importance of putting things back when you are finished using them.

During the years while I was singing, my repertoire listed 59 songs -- here are just a few to jog your memory:

"Autumn Leaves" ... "Love Is a Many-Splendored Thing" ... "Ebb Tide"... "September Song" ... "Night and Day" ... "Without a Song" ... "Blue Moon" ... "That Old Black Magic" ... "Love Letters" ... "I Surrender Dear" ... "Laura" ... "Stardust" ... "Beseme Mucho" ... "I'm In the Mood For Love" ... "Embraceable You" ... "Blueberry Hill" ... "I Only Have Eyes For You" ... "My Blue Heaven" ... "I'll Never Smile Again" ... "For Me and My Gal" ... and many more. I sure like those songs better than the noise and lyrics I hear today.

My agent at that time had a friend who worked for MCA (Music Corp. of America), recording compositions in New York City, and he arranged an audition for me. He wanted me to sign a contract, but his partner said no. I was disappointed, but later in life I could see God's hand in this, because I wasn't a Christian at the time and probably wouldn't have been able to handle all the temptations I would face. But when I did go to New York City to do commercials, Jesus Christ was at the center of my life and my thoughts were on Him and not on the beautiful women I worked with.

CHAPTER TWO

Here is how it all began:

I was on duty on the used car lot at Courtesy Chevrolet, and a woman from an advertising agency came up to me and said she thought I would make a good model (I always thought male models were a bunch of sissies), anyway I sent her a picture of me wearing a tuxedo, taken while I was singing with a band, and the agency hired me for a sweater ad in a national magazine. One thing led to another, and I was soon doing all kinds of modeling work for magazines and catalogs.

When I surrendered my life to Jesus I was still working at Courtesy Chevrolet in Penns Grove, NJ. The other salesmen were just like me, hard-drinking, foul-mouthed, told dirty jokes, etc. I walked into the showroom the morning after I had come to Christ and told them that I had become a Christian and was going to follow Jesus, and that led to the end of my career in the auto business. They sneered at me and ridiculed me -- "Billy Graham" this and that -- and undermined my efforts when I tried to sell cars, and eventually hounded me right out the door.

Two days after I had left Courtesy I was walking down the street and I said, "Nice going Lord, two days and I'm already unemployed." But God had other plans for me.

I was working at the studio in Philadelphia, posing for a magazine ad, and the photographer's assistant said, "Why don't you go to New York and do TV commercials like Tommy McGlagan?" (a fairly well-known model who had worked for the same agency). I got excited about his question and felt this could be God's leading.

Two days later I got into my car, got onto the NJ Turnpike, and drove on into the Big Apple. I walked into the Schwartz-Luskin agency where Tommy McGlagan had worked, and showed them a few ads that I had done in the Philadelphia Enquirer newspaper. We talked, and an hour later I signed a contract with their agent. As my work increased so did my income, truly the answer to my prayers.

The first year in NYC I had made fifteen commercials, which

was a record. My biggest success was the Aqua Velva After-Shave Lotion commercial with actress Mamie Van Doren. (They had tried to get Sophia Loren but she wasn't available-- boy, was I disappointed, as she is one of my favorite actresses).

We made seven different Aqua Velva commercials, which ran for 3 ½ years. Every time these were shown on TV, I received a residual payment. Needless to say I made a lot of money.

Some of the other most important commercials were M & M Candies; Gillette Razors; and Alka Seltzer; Kodak (the picture below was an ad for Kodak Cameras; it was 30 feet high and 60 feet long, and it hung in Grand Central Station for three months.) Some of the other commercials I did were Chase & Sanborn Coffee; Colgate (bad breath); Command (hair tonic);

Dristan (sinus problems); AT&T (telephones); Palmolive (soap); Sunsweet Prune Juice (constipation).People liked to talk about my Aqua Velva commercials, but never about my bad breath, body odor, or constipation commercials.

I remember shooting a Stouffer's Frozen Spinach commercial. The actress I worked with asked me how I got started in my TV career. I took her to lunch at Howard Johnson at

57th Street and Park Avenue, and explained how I became a Christian and ended up in NYC. She said she would like to know Jesus, so I introduced her to Him -- I told her that all it takes is to confess your sins and ask for forgiveness; ask Jesus to come into your heart and be your Savior; that we are all born with a sinful nature until the Holy Spirit comes to live inside you to teach you how to live with Him.

I never saw her again, so don't know what happened to her.

While I worked in New York, I attended a Bible class once a week with some top business executives. I met the editor of Guidepost magazine, who found out about my witness for Christ. The Guidepost printed an article with my story, titled "The Case of the Immature Husband." Three years later they reprinted this article, this time with pictures, about my fantastic success as one of the top TV commercial actors in the U.S. (P.T.L. -- He did it). TV Guide did an article about my fantastic success as one of the top TV commercial actors in the U.S. (P.T.L. -- He did it).

My agent sent me on an interview for a 30-day trip to South America for Pan Am Airlines. I was really excited and made plans to take Hilda with me. I sure was disappointed when I didn't get the job, but God had other plans for me.

One day my agent at the Stewart Men's Agency said that I had so many commercials running, covering so many products, that they couldn't get me any more work. She suggested that I take my family to Paris for a year or two and work in Europe.

I rushed home, burst into the house, and shouted to Hilda that we were all going to move to Europe for one or two years. She said, "We are going to do WHAT ?"

About this time Pan American Airlines sent me to Europe for 30 days to do photos for their catalog with my partner Annabel; we traveled all over Europe shooting pictures . If I had done the South America Pan Am job I wouldn't have gotten this opportunity.

Traveling to exotic foreign places, living in luxury hotels, spending time with a lovely woman, might have been a temptation in my previous life before I accepted Christ, but now I often talked with Annabel about Hilda and my kids and how much I loved them. This also helped to establish a comfortable working relationship with Annabel.

While I was in Paris, I found a perfect four-room furnished apartment for us when we would all get there. I then flew home, and walked into the house while Hilda was on the phone -- she screamed and hung up -- she thought I was still in Europe.

I arrived home from the Pan Am trip the day before our son James was going to graduate from high school. Another example of God's perfect timing was that I was there to help Hilda get all

our trunks packed and put on the S.S. France. for our trip to Europe.

We rented the house I had built on my great-grandfather's farm and sailed to Paris. Both our teenage sons were really angry with us for taking them away from their friends. They pouted all the way to Paris. Our daughter Helen was excited, but then, she wasn't yet a teenager, only 5 years old. When we got to Paris, the S.S. France delivered all our baggage to our apartment.

We bought the boys a Moped bike and subway passes and

turned them loose. It took about two days and the pouting turned into excitement when they realized what fun and adventure they were in for. We put them into private schools. We also bought a VW camper, and camped all over Europe.

My agent had it all arranged for me to go to Paris Planning (a talent agency). I walked in and told them who I was, and they told me how angry they were with me. They had booked me for two or three jobs and had to cancel them. They then booked me all over Europe -- London, Paris, Rome and Spain.

When I look back at my past I am amazed at how many countries I have traveled to and how many places Hilda, James, Keith and Helen got to visit with me.

ITALY: Rome, Pisa, Milan, Florence
GERMANY: Munich, Stuttgart, Cologne, Frankfort, Hamburg
AUSTRIA: Salsburg
SCOTLAND: Glasgow, Giga Island (where the Galbraith family originated)
ENGLAND: London, Stratford-on-Avon
HOLLAND: Amsterdam, Rotterdam
LUXEMBOURG

BELGIUM: Brussels, Brugge

FRANCE: Paris, Calais

PORTUGAL: Lisbon

SPAIN: Madrid, Barcelona

MONACO

CARIBBEAN: Nassau, Bermuda, Cayman Islands, San Juan, Puerto Rico, Caracas, Venezuela, Kingston, Jamaica, and Amway's Peter Island.

NORTH AFRICA: Algeria, Oran, Tangier, Rabat, Morocco, Mers El Kabir (this is where my ship refueled during WW II. When the crew would get liberty, we'd go ashore; we had to stick together because the Arabs were so vicious against foreigners. One time my friends agreed they wanted to go to a house of ill repute, so we ended up in there -- but at my age I was terrified to even touch anybody, as aboard ship we were shown films about venereal diseases and what they can do to you. We weren't there five minutes and the lady [madam] came running in, "The SPs are coming, the SPs (Shore Patrol) are coming" -- and we weren't supposed to be there because it was off limits to the military servicemen. The women moved a chest of drawers aside and there was a passageway leading to a hidden room; they put us in there, but five minutes later the SPs knew where it was and, BANG, they came in and then they threw us all into the brig. We all got fined $20 and 20 hours of extra duty.)

While Hilda, Helen and I were traveling through Scotland we decided to go to Gigha Island, where all the Galbraith ancestors were buried.

Gigha is a very small island, about 3 ½ miles long and 1 ½ miles wide. We went to the small church, and discovered that one of the stained glass windows was donated by Emily Galbraith.

In the graveyard, I took pictures of the tombstones; some were of sea captains. There was one tombstone telling of the Galbraith who was a pirate, and was hung. We also discovered there is no longer anyone living there with the name of Galbraith. Their descendants own a family chain of Galbraith Stores, located all over Scotland.

When the Galbraith family lived in Paris we went to the American Church of Paris, I sang in the choir, and remember singing in Handel's Messiah concert at the Paris Opera House. Audrey Hepburn also attended that church. I also started a Bible study in my home with some of the members there.

One day I was on the Metro (subway) in Paris on the way to a studio. I noticed an American couple looking at a map with confusion, and I asked if I could help them, and after I had shown them the way to go, they shared that they were from Sharptown, NJ and had attended the Methodist Church there. They told me all their relatives were buried in the church cemetery. They almost fell over when I told them I live five miles from Sharptown, and I had attended that church and sang in the choir. Not only that, but my great-grandfather Truitt Perry was buried there, and many others in my family have their final resting place there too. Small world, isn't it?

Here's another one: Later, when we were in the Amway business and were on a RAMA trip (a monthly contest where the winners got an award of a trip to a tropical country), Hilda and I were in Jamaica. We rented a jeep and drove up to the top of a mountain to a small village. A man approached us and wanted us to sponsor him so he could return to the U.S. He told us he had worked in NJ on a farm near Swedesboro for Sonja Swan, a Metropolitan Opera Star. I told him that my Uncle James and Aunt Edna had rented a house on her farm and that I had lived there with them.

And another one -- one time Hilda and I were in Morocco, North Africa, walking down the street, and came across a store that had an Aqua Velva poster in the window with my picture. Small world indeed.

Believe me, it is hard to imagine that we traveled to all those places. God sure know how to bless you when you follow Him

We lived in Europe about 18 months, then came back to the U.S. on the Queen Mary's last voyage in 1966. James and Keith were having a ball on the French Riviera, and we had told them when the ship was due to sail. All our luggage and our VW camper were on board, and the boys weren't there yet ! In two hours the ship would be gone. Hilda said, "I don't care if the ship leaves, I won't be on it unless my two sons are with me." You can imagine the dilemna I was in -- should I go with all our possessions or stay with Hilda ? The only one who wasn't worried was 7-year-old Helen.

Then it happened -- we looked down at the end of the pier and then, praise the Lord, there came James and Keith, just two hours before the ship left.

When we docked in NYC we had to go through Customs. We had four or five big suitcases and two big barrels with us. Our good friend Ann Snyder and my brother Bob were waiting on the dock to drive us home.

If you know how sweet Hilda was you can understand WHY she did WHAT she did. When she was shopping in Paris, a sales clerk gave her some perfume samples. As a gesture of thanks to the Customs Inspector she offered him some of the perfume samples to take home to his wife.

His superior overheard Hilda make this offer and thought it was a bribe and immediately gave orders to go through everything we had. It took 2 ½ hours, and my brother Bob and Ann were standing and waiting on the dock not knowing what had happened. But guess what ? We all got home to the farm safe and sound.

When we got back home from Europe I went to NYC and resumed my TV career.

One commercial was for M & M Candies, the line was "M & Ms melt in your mouth and not in your hand."

Another ad was for "Mr. Cool Men's Suits" by Clipper Craft. To get this shot of me on water skis dressed in a business suit and holding an attache' case, they put me on a sea buoy, where I put on my skis and skied slowly behind the boat. I was really a pretty good water skier, and

people in the boats that passed us just stared at me with their mouths open ! Of course the pants legs got wet and wrinkled, and later the photo was airbrushed so the suit looked perfectly smooth.

One time my agent in NYC called me and said, "We have a job for you", and gave me the address of the studio. I went there, got in the elevator with another man and a woman. We found out we were going to the same floor, where I walked up to the photographer and whispered to him, "That Lady looks a lot like Carol Burnett." He hollered, "Hey Carol, this guy thinks you look like Carol Burnett !" Well, guess what, she was!

We all had a big laugh. Carol is one of the nicest, sweetest, friendliest stars I ever met.

CHAPTER THREE

In 1961 when God started to deal with our lives, He put a young new minister and his wife, Chuck and Nancy Murray, in our path, and through them and many others whose lives were centered in Jesus Christ, He began to speak to my heart.

In my quiet time I was reading Psalms 19: 7-11 where it says, "God's Laws are perfect. They protect us, make us wise, and give us joy and light. For they warn us away from harm and give success to those who obey them." What has happened to Hilda and me and our three kids is living proof that this is true.

First Hilda surrendered herself to His care, then me, then I led my youngest son Keith to the Lord. Finally our little five-year-old daughter Helen asked Jesus to forgive her for her sins and come into her heart; and at last our son James got the message and joined God's family with us. What a changed family we became! The Murrays had more influence on me than anyone else ever had, and we've been incredible friends ever since.

Jesus said, "Seek and you will find." As we read God's word, went to church, had Christian fellowship and attended prayer groups, we started to grow, and God laid out a plan for our lives -- He richly blessed us. He took me out of the automobile business and in a matter of months I was on TV doing commercials. TV Guide published an article about my career as one of the top commercial actors in the business.

I started to saturate TV with all my commercials, especially Aqua Velva; then I was invited to speak all over the country and share how Jesus Christ really can change a person. I shared my faith in schools, universities, prisons, hospitals, churches, and was even on David Brinkley's radio show Journal -- all stemmed from people seeing me on TV. I literally gave him my testimony on how my whole life turned around and how I became a TV commercial actor.

I was ordained as an Elder in my church, taught Sunday School, sang in the choir, and started worship services in the hospital and jail. When you pray, God hears your prayers. How do you know? The Holy Spirit IS God and lives within you IF Jesus Christ is your savior; He hears not only your prayers, but what motivates you to pray.

The Bible teaches us that when we "seek the Kindom of God first in our lives all the best will be added unto us" (Matthew 6: 33, NLB). As I look back over our lives and see all the exciting things that have happened to us since Jesus took over, I'm amazed at this tremendous power and love God wants to share with each one of us if we would but let Him. The secret to success and happiness lies in the verse Luke 6:30, "Give and it shall be given unto you," following the way, the truth and the life.

Hilda and I have poured ourselves out in Europe, U.S. and Canada, sharing, giving and loving, and as a result God has shared and given and poured out His love on us. We take no credit for any good, but like everyone else in the world, we are sinners, undeserving of God's love and mercy but because He loves us so much, He sent Jesus; and we who trust Him need never to be afraid again. "God has not given us the spirit of fear, but of love, power, and a fantastic mind."

Because I was a TV personality and a Christian, I was asked to speak in a great many churches and as a leader on Christian retreats. One day I asked the Lord if He would start to use me in reaching people who didn't go to church. Well, God really answered that prayer in a very dramatic way.

Again Chuck and Nancy Murray were used by the Lord. They called us and told us about this super business they just got into. Nancy told me that Jesus had told her in her quiet time that Hilda and I were to get into this business with her. I said, "Nancy, He may have told you but He hasn't told me." Frankly I just wasn't interested -- "Here I am a star on TV and you want me to sell soap? Are you crazy ?"

Nancy would not give up and for months kept calling me. She kept saying that this Amway business was founded by two wonderful Christians, that there was no hanky-panky, and it was a way to make money by helping others. "But Jim, you can build a business and years later you can still have money coming in from it" -- (that was the truth, I get a check every month from the business I built 40 years ago).

I believe now that the Lord was using Nancy to reach me, but I wouldn't listen, so He had to intervene. While cleaning out the river bank on the farm where we lived in NJ, I cut my foot open and was on crutches and couldn't go anywhere or do anything.

"Ah-ha!" says Nancy to herself. "I gotcha Jim Galbraith, now you HAVE to sit there and see how Amway works.," and she sent her partner Dave Yolton down to me, and we met at Annabell Tuthill's house in Salem, NJ (a friend from church -- she made good iced tea and cookies when it was hot, and that was the only reason I went). Annabell had already joined Nancy in the Amway business, but I wasn't much interested as Dave unfolded this "wonderful opportunity" to me.

"But Dave," I said, "I have a great career on TV, why should I go into another business?" When he finally got to the end of his presentation he showed me a way I could build a part-time business that in time could give me a permanent income. All of a sudden I had my eyes opened, because this would give me a chance to go into full-time Christian outreach. (At that time I hadn't planned on leaving my TV business.)

Needless to say, Hilda and I got into the Amway business. Being very uncertain what we were doing, we asked Jesus to be out business partner.

Our business started to grow really fast, and one day we were asked to speak at an Amway rally and share how we became successful. As I was speaking to these excited people, Hilda and I shared with them how much Jesus had been a part of not only our marriage, but our business as well.

After that meeting I realized that God had indeed answered my prayer. We were speaking to a great many people who never went to church or any Christian function, and sharing the love of the Lord with them. At that moment I knew the Lord had opened a whole new ministry for Hilda and me.

RICH DE VOS and JAY ANDEL (deceased) started their Amway business in JAY's home in the basement. Amway is now a multi-billion dollar business.

When Hilda and I were on another Amway RAMA trip we sailed all over the Caribbean Sea, even down to Caracas, Venezuela. Aboard the ship with us were Rich De Vos, founder of Amway Corp., and our friends Dick and Dee Ossinger

Rich asked me if I would conduct a church service on Sunday; it's pretty hard to say no to Rich. We met in the ship's bar room. Dick was sitting next to

Richard M. De Vos
President

Jay Van Andel
Chairman of the Board

Rich, and when I was talking, he kept slapping Dick on his leg, saying, "Isn't that great ?" Dick said when he left that his leg was sore.

I have so many exciting stories to tell I can't stop myself ! When I worked in NYC I had the same theatrical agent as Rob Roy; we had worked

together in Philadelphia doing print ads. One day we were sitting in my car talking, and I told him I had to go to a warehouse to get some things. He asked, "What for ?" and I told him I had just

gotten into a new business. He said he would be interested in hearing about it, so one night he and his wife Linda drove all the way down from Chalfort, PA, to our farm in southern NJ. When they heard about our business they wanted to join Hilda and me in Amway (When they left our house there was about 1½ feet of snow on their car roof).

They became the biggest and best distributors we ever had; in fact we still receive a bonus check every month from the business they started 30 years ago.

Rob was a tall handsome guy with a beautiful wife and two wonderful daughters, Gwenny and Cynthia. Rob was a lot like me (as I used to be). He was always on the prowl for his next conquest.

Hilda and I invited them to be our guests at Jerome Hines' opera "I Am The Way" which Jerome wrote, at the Metropoligan Opera House. It was terrific. He played the part of Jesus. Afterwards there was a reception at the Bellevue Stratford Hotel ballroom.

I did something I had never done before, because I knew Rob inside and out -- I used to be just like him. I got right in his face and said, "Rob, it's about time you stop fooling around and get your life straightened out before you lose Linda and your daughters." I looked him right in the eye and said, "You need Jesus Christ and you need Him right now." I never saw anyone squirm and hem and haw like he did. After about five minutes the fight went out of him, and he became a new creature in Christ Jesus.

Now watch this: Across the dance floor Rob's wife Linda was doing the same thing he had just done. Leading her to Jesus was Millie Dienert, the wife of Fred Dienert, who was Billy Graham's publicity director. Rob and Linda led their daughters to Christ,

and put them in good schools and colleges. The four of them went out and shared their faith everywhere --Rob played the trombone, Linda played the piano, and both daughters sang.

Here's another example of God leading me -- Years ago in Philadelphia the evangelist Billy Graham was conducting one of his famous Crusades. I lived in Philadelphia at the time and decided to go and see if I could meet him. After the program was over, I went backstage and I was blessed to meet and talk to the wonderful man of God.

Also backstage I met Cliff Barrows, who has been with the Graham team since its beginning. Cliff is the Master of Ceremonies and also lead singing. We got along just great; a friendship bond was formed that night.

Several years later Cliff wrote to me and asked if I could join the team for dinner before the Crusade started in London, England. I just"happened" to be in London at the time shooting a commercial.

There I was at the Holiday Inn in London having a steak dinner with Cliff Barrows, Ruth Graham and George Beverly Shay (who has been with the team as their soloist since the beginning, and introduced for the first time the very popular hymn "How Great Thou Art").

Talk about being blessed and favored ! All I can say is "Praise the Lord"as he is the One who arranged the whole thing. It was a very humbling and truly wonderful experience for me. P.T.L.

CHAPTER FOUR

One summer Hilda and I took the boys up to Canada on a vacation and rented two cabins on a lake. We ate all our meals in the dining room.

I rented a boat and went out fishing, threw my line into the water, and caught a 4-pound walleye pike. I took it to the dining room and they cooked it for us. I really got hooked on fishing after that vacation.

When we got home again I decided I wanted to build a cabin there.

Not much later I went back, and found a Christian realtor who took me around to a lot of different lakes. I found the one I liked, and he let me use his boat. I rowed across the lake, cast my line out, and on the first cast I had hit and pulled in a big walleyed pike. That reminded me of what Jesus did -- He told Peter to go cast his line in the lake, and on the first cast he hooked a fish, opened its mouth, and there was a coin that Jesus used to pay the temple tax.

I then bought this beautiful property with 525 feet of lake front.

I went home and told Hilda and she said "You did WHAT?" Every time I have told Hilda my plans it scared her. But moving to Canada -- moving to Paris -- building a cottage -- she has always been glad after we got there. She has been a great partner who always supported and encouraged me in all that I have done (since I became a Christian).

The Lord led us to Canada, and we moved to Belleville, Ontario and settled down there. We had rented our NJ farmhouse and eventually sold it.

Our plan was to build the Amway business in Canada and to be close to our cottage on Schwenagog Lake. We had a beautiful three-bedroom cottage with kitchen, dining room and living room with a spectacular view of the lake.

We had a pontoon boat, and one time one of my best friends, Jim Davis, and I were cruising around the lake looking for some driftwood.

I had made some lamps from drift-wood. At the end of the lake we found a trail, so we got out and explored it. It led us to an old Indian trapper's cabin, with  a rotten roof, no doors, and the two windows were gone. It also had a dirt floor.

We numbered all the logs and loaded them onto the Queen Mary (our name for the pontoon boat) and took it back to our property. We put it all together, bought and installed two windows and the door. We put up the roof and covered it with cedar shingles, then put in a wooden floor, built a bunk bed, and installed a wood stove and chimney.

I used to go up there on my Ski-doo in the winter, shovel  1½ to 2 feet of snow off the roof of the cabin and shovel my way into the door. I would then start a fire in the wood stove and in about an hour it was nice and cozy. Cooking my steak and potatoes in that stove was great.

We started our Amway business, and three years later it had spread coast to coast. This became so successful that Amway took Hilda and me in their corporate jet plane to speak in all the major cities in Canada and the U.S. at their Amway rallies and share our testimony about how Amway and Jesus had changed our lives.

The Executive Director of Amway in Canada, Frank Wilson, flew with us. We shared our story with him and gave him a Bible to read. He wrote to us later to let us know he had turned his life over to Jesus. Thank God he did, because shortly after that he died and went to be with the Lord -- the point is that if he hadn't made that commitment he would not be in Heaven now. You can figure out where he would be.

Real miracles, changed lives and new hope have all been the results of many of these people realizing that God really does know and care for them, that He has a plan for their lives if they would but seek Him.

Hilda and I have given out hundreds of New Testaments to searching, lost people. We have shared our story from Boston to San Francisco, and from Vancouver to Nova Scotia.

All these wonderful experiences happened to us because we were willing to let God use us. He did it all. We have found the answer to real happiness lies in the Scriptures verse Luke 6:38, "Give and it shall be given unto you; pressed down and shaken together and running over, shall men give unto your bosom." We gave and gave and God multiplied it all back to us.

We liked Canada so much we lived there for four years.

I remember catching a lot of walleyes and filleting them. I had a big stainless steel pan and I would cover the bottom of the pan with butter, lay the fillets on top of the butter and cover them with sliced lemons, sliced onions, peppers, garlic salt and pepper, then cover the whole pan with aluminum foil. I put a hole in the top to let the steam out. I had a fireplace with a grill and put the pan on it. When the fish started to cook, the aroma that came out of that hole was mouth-watering. We served it with French bread and salad.

Annabell Tuthill's husband Jay was the head of Mannington Mills engineering department in Salem, NJ. Jay did not like fish and never ate it *until* he ate my walleye dish. He went back three times for more.

[Their son Robby, who is a spirit-filled Christian, called me in August 2006. He told me how Hilda and I had influenced his life. He said that God had been revealing to him that He had something really big and exciting for Jim Galbraith's future. I was then 80 years old and had my doubts. One Sunday my Pastor, John Nocera told about Moses' ministry that didn't start until he was 80. When I told Robby I was going to write a book he said, "See, I told you."]

I can't tell you how many friends from church and from our Amway business stayed at the cottage and were blessed.

Years ago I had sponsored Bill and Verda Linn in the Amway business. They lived in Fayetteville, NC, and I had the privilege of introducing them to Jesus. Bill was a full Colonel in the para-troops and had fought in three wars. They came up to our cottage and brought their son Steve and his girlfriend.

Bill wanted me to baptize him in our lake. We got into the water and I said, "I baptize you in the name of the Father, the Son and the Holy Ghost." Bill then took a deep breath and went backwards towards the water, but he had so much air in his lungs I couldn't get him under the water, so I had to sit on him. When he came up we all started to laugh really hard. We have never heard of a baptism like that one.

[On Dec 2, 2006 I received a phone call from Bill Linn's daughter Hazel that Bill had died and went to be with the Lord. Hazel was there holding his hand when the Holy Spirit took Bill home. He was 86, and he and his family have been our friends for 40 years. He was  laid out in his uniform and received full military honors at his funeral.]

Now this story is also unimaginable. You can't tell me that God doesn't play an active part in our lives. Thirty years ago in Belleville, Hilda and I used to have Bible studies in our home with our Amway distributors. Hank and Margaret Demark came. One night I challenged them to get on board, surrender their lives and control over to Jesus. However, over the years we had lost touch with them. Now here is where you can see God's hand at work.

Please pray for
Hank and Margaret Demark

New Tribes Mission of Canada
Box 707
Durham, ON N0G 1R0
www.ntmc.ca

New Tribes Mission
1000 East First St.
Sanford, FL
32771
www.ntm.org

Home Address
274 South St. W
Box 78
Durham, ON N0G 1R
(519) 369-227
E-mail: hmdemark@wightman.c

We had not heard from the Demarks for 32 years. They had called Amway to get our phone number, and Amway then called us to ask if it was okay to give them our number. We said yes, and immediately the phone rang. They said they were strongly led to call us and thank us for the influence we had on their lives (it was the Holy Spirit, not us). For 26 years they have been missionaries with the New Tribes Mission, and have been all over the world. They go into a country or village with their salvation message, learning the language to blend right in with the culture and share the gospel.

Their daughter is also a missionary wih the New Tribes Mission in New Guinea, and their son Adam teaches the New Tribes Mission College.

Bob and Connie Marx are another exciting couple who were in the Amway business with Hilda and me. They also attended our Bible study and became Christians there. At that time Bob was a professor at the University of Washington. Now they are missionaries in South America, working with homeless children.

Hilda and I have given out hundreds of New Testaments to searching, lost people. We have shared our story from Boston to San Francisco, and from Vancouver to Nova Scotia. Real miracles, changed lives and new hope have all been the results of many people realizing that God really does know and care for them, that He has a plan for their lives if they would but seek Him. All these wonderful experiences happened to us because we were willing to let God use us. He did it all. We have found the answer to real happiness lies in the Scripture verse Luke 6:38, "Give and it shall be given unto you; pressed down and shaken together and running over, shall men give unto your bosom." We gave and gave and God multiplied it all back to us.

CHAPTER FIVE

The Canadian winters were so cold and damp that Hilda's bronchitis got worse every year, and I decided we must move to a warmer climate.

One time James and I went up to the cottage on the Ski-doo. We were out walking on the lake (on the ice that is). James said, "Dad, you should move out of the small town where you live, and go where the action is for your Amway business."

At the same time I was talking to Gerry Pounds, a good friend from church at Belleville. He told me about Seattle, WA and what a beautiful city it was. He and his wife Marian had been up in the Space Needle with its  wonderful view. He told me that they and their three kids were going to move to Seattle. I was convinced that we should make the move too.

I told Hilda that we were going to move to Seattle, and she said, "We are going to do WHAT ?"

A few days later I got on a plane to Seattle, rented a car, and drove to the Cosmopolitan Hotel in downtown Seattle. I flipped open the yellow pages of the phone book to the real estate section. I closed my eyes, put my finger on the name of a real estate agent who just happened to be a Christian. I told her just what I wanted, a big house, room for a garden, a view of Lake Washington, and Christian neighbors. Guess what?

She showed me a house that had all that was on my list.

The problem was the house was too big, 5100 square feet. I really wanted to buy that beautiful home, but what would we do with all that space ? Back to the hotel. I just opened my Bible, hoping there was an answer to my dilemma. I "just happened" to turn to Isaiah 54: 2, "Enlarge your house; build on additions, spread out your home ! For soon you will be bursting at the seams!" (L.B.) So guess what I did ? I picked up the phone and called the realtor and said "SOLD !" I then called Hilda and told her I had just bought a 5100 square-foot home.

She said, "You did WHAT ??? "

When I came home, we arranged to rent our cottage; then we got all our furniture into a moving van, loaded up our VW van, and hit the road !

We drove from Belleville, Ontario to Kenmore, WA. The big mistake I made was that I pushed myself to get to Seattle to show Hilda the beautiful home we had just bought. What I should have done was to go sightseeing all across America. We got there ten days before our furniture. DUMB !!

What happened next was our son Keith, his wife Leah and their two daughters Jessica and Juliana and their dog, and our daughter Helen moved to Seattle and stayed with us at the "Galbraith Hotel" until they could find a place to live.

At the same time Gerry and Marian Pounds, their three kids and their dog moved in too, until *they* could find a place to live. So we were literally "bursting at the seams" (Remember Isaiah 54: 2-3).

40

Then our Amway business took off and we had packed-out meetings in our huge downstairs recreation room.

At the time we were supplying Cherry Boone O'Neal, Pat Boone's daughter, with Amway products for her business. One night Pat came to speak at our Amway group -- you could hardly get in the front door! Hilda and I ended up using every foot of that 5100 square foot house.

Talk about "bursting at the seams."

Cherry's husband Don O'Neal con- tacted Pat Robertson's TV show, the 700 Club, and told them about me. They flew me to their studios in Virginia as a guest and they taped the program. Sitting in the audience were my daughter Helen and her new husband Jeffrey Troutt, and Col Bill Linn and his wife Verda. The host Ben Kinslow interviewed me, and started talking about my commercials for Aqua Velva, saying, "There's something about an Aqua Velva man, Jim, what is that about an Aqua Velva man ?" I said, "I don't know, you'll have to ask Hilda." And that is where I got the title for this book.

I mentioned my daughter Helen being in the audience, and Ben interviewed her too, and she gave her wonderful testimony about when she was in high school in Belleville how she got mixed up with the crowd of kids who drank and smoked. She talked about how she turned against Jesus, prayer, her parents, and all she had learned as a child, and then what happened in Paris when she changed her life to follow Christ with her brother Keith and his wife Leah in their ministry. (Read her story below.)

After that, at the end, I sang this song, "Praise the Lord", with a piano accompanist. I had a terrible sore throat and was afraid I wouldn't be able to sing, but I prayed to the Lord, and it was the best that I had ever sung.

Our daughter was a wonderful child to raise. she and I used to build forts, go fishing, and I remember her sitting on my lap steering the car in our lane. The only time she gave us any trouble was when she went to public high school in Belleville. Up until then we had home-schooled her or put her in private Christian schools. Her life turned all around when she later joined her brother Keith and his ministry in Paris.

I would like you to think back to what a drunken bum and adulterer I was in June 1961 and see what happened to our kids over the past 45 years.

Our youngest son Keith married Leah Mercer in Sept 1971, and they went to Europe to attend the Sorbonne University as a part of their college education, and while in Paris met some people who led them right out of the Sorbonne into a full-time ministry that has led them all over Europe, witnessing to the dropouts and drifting people who have lost their way.

In 1978 Hilda and I flew over to Paris to spend Christmas with them and observe their work We took along a very unhappy mixed-up, hate-filled daughter. Helen was 16 ½ years old; she had turned on us and rejected anything to do with the Bible, prayer and Jesus. It all started when she entered high school when we were living in Belleville. Before that we were very close and had a great fellowship with the Lord. Then she got in with the wrong crowd and started smoking and drinking and lying to us. She was very unhappy with herself and filled with guilt, and that caused her to turn on us and reject all we stood for. There was absolutely nothing we could do. We were helpless, and we called out to Jesus for a miracle.

Then the most dramatic, exciting, positive miracle and answer to our prayer in all the years we have been Christians occurred in Paris !

Just as we were ready to leave to come home Helen came to us and asked if she could stay with Keith and Leah, not just for a month but for good. We asked her why and she said she loved their ministry and what they were doing, and wanted to become a part of it. We told her it wouldn't be easy, and Keith tried to talk her out of it, but she was convinced she didn't want to go back to the mess she had left, so with our blessing we left here there.

She wrote us long letters of how much she loved us and Jesus. She was playing the guitar and singing, and led many teenagers to the Lord.

She, Keith and Leah and our two precious granddaughters, Jessica and Juliana were all working together out of Copenhagen, Denmark.

(Jessica was born in Troy, NY and Juliana was born in Paris.)

Our oldest son Jim Jr. was working in Atlanta, GA, still single then, and trying to find out what God wanted him to do.

When Keith, Leah and Helen returned to the U.S., they settled in El Paso, TX, where Keith became an associate pastor of a Bible-centered church there, Centro Vida.

Here Helen met a law student, Jeffrey Troutt, and they fell in love. Jeffrey had long hair and played the guitar in the church band. I remember taking Jeffrey to dinner in Juarez, Mexico to talk about his relationship with Helen, and he then asked my permission to marry her.

COOL !

They then moved to Juneau, AK where Jeffrey joined a law firm to practice law. Imagine, an honest Christian lawyer (that's a joke, son).

It wasn't long before Helen was ordained as an Elder in their church. She also sings on the worship team, and is involved in the worship ministry. Helen also created the "Connections" minis-

try, a program developed to draw new Christians into the church and get them connected and discipled within the Body of Christ.

Can you imagine how thrilling it is to watch your own daughter and son be so used by God ?

Another thrilling part of Jim's and Hilda's lives was when we watched our son Keith, with his fabulous wife Leah at his side, become Director of the Family Renewal Shelter in 1990, a very tough ministry, rescuing abused women and their children who have been beaten and sometimes almost killed by husbands or partners. You couldn't believe some of the people and stories they have dealt with. Their daughters Jessica, Juliana and Emily have all been involved at different times in the Shelter's work. They recently celebrated the Shelter's 20th anniversary.

They have three shelters in secret locations, so the perpetrators cannot find their victims. An instructor is available to teach the women self-defense. an on-call dentist provides necessary dental work. There is a car repair shop. If a resident doesn't have a car, one will be supplied. Now and then the Shelter will send a resident on a train or bus to an out-of-state location to escape a very dangerous situation. The Shelter also has Bible study and prayer available; it isn't required, but many women attend and are blessed, and have come to know Jesus Christ as their personal Savior.

Family Renewal Shelter has received many letters and phone calls from previous residents all over the country, thanking them for helping get their lives back again. Keith is in demand as a speaker all the time in churches, clubs, etc. He has been interviewed many times on radio and TV. F.R.S. also has its own office building. One of the biggest assets Keith has is Leah. God knew what He was doing when He gave Leah to Keith and Hilda to Jim.

Keith's and Leah's twin sons Micah and Ethan have grown tall and strong; Micah married the beautiful Rachel on July 24, 2005 and they are a perfect "love-struck" couple. Ethan is in the waiting mode -- waiting for the perfect girl God wants him to have. Their other son Benjamin Keith (I call him B.K.) is my buddy -- he recently graduated from high school; he is big, tall and handsome. All three grandsons hug and kiss me (very rare in this world today).

Hilda and I had often thought about the different paths our sons' lives had taken. Keith dedicated his life to serving the Lord, while James' life was centered on the world, the flesh, and the devil. He had committed his heart to the Lord when he was a teenager, but he chose not to live up to that commitment. He became an alcoholic and a womanizer (sounds a lot like me before my own commitment). Hilda and I prayed for him every day for 20 years; finally we prayed, "Whatever it takes Lord, we want him to come back to you. Just the thought of James spending eternity in hell was more than we could bear, God did answer our whatever-it-takes prayer in a very dramatic way.

James lived in Atlanta, GA. He developed blood clots in his leg and was rushed to the hospital and came very close to dying.

He was sent home; and again had another blood clot emergency and was in the hospital. The doctor told him if he had gotten

there one hour later he would have been dead. I think this was a real wake-up call for him.

God put a wonderful Christian woman into his life. She started to take care of him, shopping for groceries, cooking, and cleaning his apartment. They used to spend hours talking about the Bible, Jesus and Heaven, and James recommitted his life to the Lord.

In 2000, for a third time he was rushed to the hospital. A nurse called us and told us that he would not be coming home from there. His brother Keith, sister Helen, and Hilda and I decided to fly to Atlanta before he died. I remember standing at the ticket counter at the airport with my credit card ready to buy our tickets. Helen's cell phone rang, with a message to call the hospital, and they told her that James had died. The nurse and chaplain said that he had died in perfect peace; the chaplain was certain he had gone to be with the Lord in Heaven. James was 52 years old.

We decided not to fly to Atlanta, because James was gone -- the trip would be useless.

We had James cremated and his ashes sent to us. Keith, Leah, Helen, Jeffrey, Hilda and I went to a park on Puget Sound. We prayed and thanked God for the assurance that we knew that James was with Jesus; we then scattered his ashes in the water, knowing that we would all see him again. Praise the Lord.

The Galbraith Family, 1962

CHAPTER SIX

Our new home in Kenmore, WA was about one mile from Dick and Dee Ossinger's estate. Dick had lost both of his eyes, but being blind didn't stop him. He and Dee built their Amway business to the highest level you can go, Crown Direct. They too flew on Amway's jet plane and have spoken all over the country. What an inspiration they are; they became our dear friends.

One day the Ossingers asked their Amway distributors to come over and help them clean up and get moved into their new home. I had brought my chain saw and Dick asked me if I would cut down a willow tree hanging over their driveway, so I cut it down and it fell right over their driveway  (there was no other place it could fall). I then turned to Dick and told him I had to leave. He said, "You mean you are just going to leave that tree there ?"

I said, "I'll tell you what! If you and Dee promise to go to church every Sunday I'll cut up the tree." They agreed, and have been going to church every Sunday since then. Jesus Christ became the center of their lives. (I just talked to Dee and she was on her way out to her Bible class, praise the Lord !).

One day the Ossingers were having a celebration at their home and they asked me to be a host along with Senator J.T. Quigg of Washington State, and greet Dick and Dee's Amway distributors as they arrived. Senator Quigg knew I was a patriot and told me I should run for an open seat in the House of Representatives as a Republican in 1984. After praying about it, I said yes and jumped into the race. With much affirmation and Scripture I knew this was what God would have me do.

When I lost the race after about 14 months, I was very confused. Why did God want me to run knowing I wouldn't win?

Here is the answer: During my campaign there were many people involved in my race who believed in me. So with about 30 people, we started "FACTS FOR FREEDOM" -- Faith, Action, Commitment, Truth, Stability. Our purpose was to research the issues, i.e. what was going on in the government in Washington, our State capitol Olympia, schools, our courts, and the media and send out our *ACTION*GRAM, informing Christian conservatives churches and families what is happening that will affect them, and giving suggestions of what they could do about it -- issues they will never learn from our ultra-liberal media.

FACTS also researches the candidates at each election and publishes FACTS Election Endorsement list, for the past 22 years. Most Christians and pastors don't have a clue about who they should vote for. That is why thousands of copies are made and distributed throughout the State.

Every months FACTS has a conservative speaker come and address issues we are concerned about, including Washington State Attorney General Rob McKenna, Senators such as Val Stevens (past president of Washington State Concerned Women of America); Peter Marshall, author of "The Light and the Glory"; Dr. Paul Cameron of Washington D.C. "Research on Homosexuality" (at that meeting the homosexuals came out in force to protest); Leo Thorsness, pilot, prisoner of war, Medal of Honor winner;

U.S. Senate candidate Debra Ray, author of "ABCs of Globalism" and "ABCs of Culturalism"; David Barton, "U.S. History and the Constitution"; Richard Sanders, Supreme Court Justice; Bill Goodloe, Supreme Court Justice; Bill and Kathy Swan, who were unjustly jailed for four years for alleged rape of their five-year-old daughter; Pastor W. Keith Galbraith, Executive Director of Family Renewal Shelter; Frosty Fowler, talk show host; John Carlson, talk show host, "Three Strikes, You're Out"; Howard Phillip, Presidential Candidate for the U.S. Taxpayer Party; , talk show host Kirby Wilbur; Congressman John Miller (he is the one who defeated me in my run for Congress, praise the Lord); Azis Sadat, on Afghanistan and the Russian invasion.

The list goes on and on. We've been holding these monthly meetings, sending out our monthly newsletter *ACTION*GRAM and our FACTS endorsement sheet for 22 years. Can you see why God didn't want me to win my race for Congress ?

At one of our FACTS rally we invited Dr. Paul Cameron from Washington, D.C. as a guest speaker. He spoke about his book, "AIDS and Sexuality" and his research on AIDS and homosexuality. Before the meeting even started, the homosexuals called all the media, announcing that 200 to 300 of them would come out in force to protest. The M.C., Bob Anderson, warned them that if they acted up they would be put out. Only 30 showed up. But guess who did show up in force ? All the local TV news channels; there were cameras set up all over the place, as well as reporters from the Seattle Times and Post-Intelligencer, all eager for a wild juicy story.

I asked them why they were there, and they said they wanted to hear what Dr. Cameron had to say. When Bob introduced him, all the cameras were trained on him; five minutes later all the cameras turned around and focused on the homosexuals who, as if on cue, started to holler and curse. The police were outside, and Bob called them in and had the protesters removed, and the meeting went on as scheduled.

Shortly after this meeting, the threats started. I was at home; the phone rang, a man asked if I was Jim Galbraith, did I live at so-and-so address? I said yes, and he said he was just checking, as he didn't want to burn down the wrong house.

Later I was speaking in a large church in Everett, and I shared the above story with the audience. After the service the pastor, who was sitting in the front row, came up to me and said (you may find this hard to believe, I know I did), "While you were speaking I saw an 8-foot angel with a sword standing beside you. He told me to tell you not to worry, that he would protect you." I didn't know whether to believe him or not, until a man ran up from the back of the church to the pastor and me and said, "Did you see him too ?" All doubts I had were gone, and I truly believe there is an 8-foot-angel with a sword who watches over me. The other man gave him a Scripture for me, that I am doing God's will, and that He is pleased with me. WOW !! Psalm 91: 10-11; "How then can evil overtake me or any plague come near me ? For He orders His angels to protect me wherever I go." And Hebrews 1: 14; "The angels are only spirit messengers sent to help and care for those who are ready to receive His salvation."

I REALLY BELIEVE IN ANGELS !! DO YOU ??

My good friend Jesse Long asked me to come and speak at the Bread of Life Mission in downtown Seattle. Jesse was on the Board of Directors. The Bread of Life has been there for 62 years, reaching out to the homeless street people. They are served breakfast, sandwiches and coffee for lunch, and every night a terrific dinner. Before dinner, the Mission has someone speak about the importance of eternal life.

When I speak at their chapel, my message is that all of us will live forever -- where we spend eternity, in Heaven or in hell, is up to us. Through the years I have seen hundreds turn their lives over to the Lord, and I will be spending eternity with them in Heaven. Those that come to the Lord can stay at the Mission for three months for training, getting ready to go back into the world armed with faith and help from the Lord, and help in finding a job.

One of the most exciting ministries I have been involved with has been in the Bread of Life Chapel as I watch God come alive and see lives changed. I also served on the Board of Directors.

In 1985 I was given the honor of serving as President of the Young Men's Republican Club in downtown Seattle, speaking to leaders. It was founded in 1900. They meet every Monday for lunch, and once a year host a banquet with very special speakers. To give you an idea of HOW special, here are some of their names: Warren Harding; President Dwight D. Eisenhower; President Gerald Ford; President Richard Nixon; and California Governor Ronald Reagan; in 1983 at the YMRC meeting Governor Reagan announced he would be running for U.S. President in 1984.

In 1985 President Reagan started his Strategic Defense Initiative (SDI) program, or as the media labeled it, "Star Wars", a system that would shoot down any incoming missiles aimed at the U.S.

The Soviet Union realized they couldn't compete with the U.S. and that the SDI could block their threat of attacking the U.S. with their nuclear bombs. Many believe this was the beginning of the breakdown of the Soviet Union.

President Reagan had appointed LtGen Don Graham to head up the SDI program, and I was able to invite him to come and speak at our YMRC banquet. What an eye-opener his story was!

President Reagan invited me and other top Christian political active leaders to attend a conference at the White House of the leaders of Christian political organizations from all across America, to discuss my Christian FACTS FOR FREEDOM ministry (among other subjects); Howard Baker, his Chief of Staff, was also there. What an honor.

I became good friends with Supreme Court Justice William Goodloe during President Reagan's administration. At the time he was running for the U.S. Senate in Washington State. One day he called me and said that wherever he goes campaigning, people ask him if he is a Christian and does he read the Bible. He said, "Yes, I am a Christian and I read the Bible every day." They asked him if he is born again; he didn't know how to answer them. I then told him what that means, that we are born once physically and we are dead spiritually, ever since Adam and Eve sinned and God withdrew from the garden of Eden and left them on their own.

God has a plan on how we can get back into fellowship with Him. He sent His own Son to become the one and only perfect sacrifice, when He shed His blood and was murdered on that cross. What made His crucifixion perfect was that Jesus was perfect and never committed a sin. I said, "So Bill, all that is needed is for you to confess your sins, ask for forgiveness, and invite Jesus to come into your heart. When you do that God send His Holy Spirit to live in your heart, and that is what is meant to be born again."

Bill said, "Jim, I have been a good man all my life." I answered, "If being good could get us into Heaven, why did Jesus have to die?"

Then I led him to the Lord over the phone. He later was a speaker at our FACTS rally, and he said, "Before I start, I've got something very exciting to share with you," he raised his hands in the air and said, "I've just met Jesus and He's totally turned my life around. My daughter has been praying for me for years to come to Christ, and it happened and I'm so happy !"

The judge had examined the facts and made his decision; it wasn't much longer after that when he died; Bill Goodloe is in Heaven right now with his Lord and Savior.

In John 3:15 Jesus said, "Anyone who believes in me will have eternal life. For God loved the world so much that He gave His only Son so that anyone who believes in Him shall not perish but have eternal life. God did not send His Son into the world to condemn it, but to save it."

There is no eternal doom awaiting those who trust Him to save them. But those who don't trust Him have already been tried and condemned for not believing in the only Son of God (John 3:18, L.B.).

AND THAT 'S THE BOTTOM LINE !!!

CHAPTER SEVEN

In 1997 Hilda and I were having Thanksgiving dinner at Keith's and Leah's house. They asked us to come into their bedroom as they had something to tell us. Keith said, "Dad, you and Mom are getting up in years, and if anything happened to either one of you, we are so far away we couldn't be much help to you." They suggested we move down near them in Tacoma.

So I contacted their good friend Kris Malang, a realtor who had helped them when they needed a house and office building. I told her what we would want in a home. She made some suggestions and I drove down to take a look. I was disappointed and went home to tell Hilda that we were not going to move. We loved the house we were in, and the town. So I dropped the whole idea.

We lived right next to the Bayside Community Church, and Pastor Scott Montague and Pastor Brent Hierschy were our good friends. Months later I was in their office, and they were discussing plans to cut down the trees between our house and the church building. They also went into details of getting rid of the beautiful lawn and putting in 150 parking spaces. That did it! We were going to move.

Now watch this: The very next day the phone rang and it was Kris Malang, who told me about a friend of hers who was going to rent his brand new home. It was on five acres with a beautiful barn, and the rent was only $1000 a month. All I had to do was take care of his seven ponies that he used to pull a carousel. Our landlord in Kingston was going to raise our rent the next month to $1450. The lease was on my desk ready to sign. (We had sold our home in Kenmore and now rented a house in Kingston.)

I met Keith the next day and I fell in love with the place. Hilda was thrilled too. Keith couldn't get over the place and how low the rent was. Isn't God's timing perfect? We not only found a beautiful new home but saved $5400 a year in rent.

Another bonus we received was that our landlord Everett Bottemiller has become our dear friend and has bent over backwards to bless us.

When we moved to Tacoma, Pastors Scott Montague and Brent Heirschy recommended that we attend the Summit Christian Church, where Scott was the youth pastor. We did go, and the church had about 30 people in the service.

Dr. John Nocera had just started as the new pastor; John has two doctorates in theology, and his wife Vivian has a doctorate in counseling, and is now the children's ministry director. The church started to grow and now there are two services; about 250 people attend this Bible-teaching, spirit-filled church.

John has become a very dear friend of mine. He conducted memorial services for both my son James and my wife Hildy. At both services, another friend, Ernie Harris, superbly played the piano. Ernie is one of the best worship leaders I know.

Here is the key to Jim, Hilda and our families abundant life: Matthew 6: 33 -- "Seek you first the Kingdom of God and all these things (the abundant life) will be added unto you."

After we had come to the Lord in 1961, every morning Hilda and I would have our breakfast together. I would research what was happening in our government, culture, school, the media, etc. on the issues that would affect Christians, the family, and conservatives; and since 1984, for my Facts For Freedom *ACTION-GRAM* newsletter. Then I would explain to Hilda how a lot of what is happening today ties into Jesus' teaching on the end days (read Matthew 24 and Luke 21, and the prophesies that haven't been fulfilled yet about Jesus' second coming). All the prophecies about His first coming HAVE been fulfilled in minute detail.

Then we would study God's word and discuss what it means in relation to the world and our life today. Hilda and I always had a fervent prayer time together and saw many of our prayers answered. This was the foundation we built our lives on, Jesus and God's Word.

Being a Christian docsn't necessarily mean life is all joy and happiness.

Along life's journey we all will have trials tribulations and heartaches.

The good news is that Christians have someone to turn to who will see us through the rough times in our lives. Jesus said, "Cast your burdens upon me because I care for you." (I Peter 5: 7)

One of the major burdens of my life took place on Jan 15, 2006. For more than 1 ½ years my precious wife of 60 years had suffered from Alzheimer's disease. She was 86 years old. It is very difficult to watch the love of your life slowly lose almost all her memories. She had also broken her hip and had to have surgery. Afterwards she suffered intense pain. Her family visited her often, and I went to see her every day to feed her lunch, sing hymns with her, and read her God's Word.

One day the nurse took me aside and said that Hilda was fading fast and that her organs had started to shut down. Our son Keith and our son-in-law Jeffrey from Juneau AK stayed with her 24 hours a day for three days. The nurse brought a mattress and they slept on the floor.

I walked into Hilda's room and they asked me if I would stay with Mom while they went out for about 45 minutes. While I was sitting there beside Hilda's bed, I put my hand on her chest and could feel a rumbling there. She was staring straight up toward the ceiling with her eyes wide open. She then took a deep breath and closed her eyes as the Holy Spirit took her to be with Jesus, and her son James, her mother, father, two brothers and two sisters.

That had to be one of the happiest moments of my life as I was there with her when she left her sick, broken, worn-out body and went immediately to be with her Lord and Savior.

Instead of mourning, I am rejoicing ! All I have to do is remember where Hilda is and with whom. Of course I miss her -- it isn't easy to adjust to living alone. Thank God I am surrounded by my loving family.

Hilda left behind her husband Jim, her son Keith Galbraith and his wife Leah, their daughter Jessica and her husband David Gray (who is a professional artist whose paintings sell for big bucks), their two kids Loren Sky and Forrest; granddaughter Julianna Galbraith (who is the manager of the Family Renewal Shelter, a tough job); twin grandsons Micah and Ethan Galbraith, and Benjamin Galbraith; granddaughter Emily and her husband Bryce Wegner, and their two kids, Kellon and Addison.

Micah and Ethan are avid fishermen, just like me. They are both "people" persons, very friendly, and everyone likes them, especially Rachel, Micah's wife. They were married at our horse farm outside in the meadow with the woods as a background.

B.K. loves riding his bicycle; however, he had an accident on it and broke his leg; cast, crutches, the whole nine yards. He had to have surgery on his knee, very painful. Knowing B.K., he will be right back on his bike.

In addition, our daughter Helen A. Galbraith Troutt has a terrific husband, Jeffrey, who is Deputy Director, Division of

There are now 23 in the Galbraith family living on this planet

Insurance for the State of Alaska. They have three beautiful daughters: Britany lives in Hollywood, is a professional dancer and a cheerleader for the Los Angeles Clippers basketball team; her sister Ashley is going to acting school, right now she works for a helicopter company in Juneau; last summer she got me a free ride on a helicopter so I could walk around on a glacier on top of the mountain -- WOW ! Rebecca just graduated from high school and is a collector of all kinds of pets; no doubt she would be a fine veterinarian.

The exciting part is that Hilda and James are waiting for us to join them in Heaven. Except for the three infants, all have accepted Jesus Christ as their Savior. Remember that old hymn?

"When we all get to Heaven, what a wonderful day that will be, when we all see Jesus we'll sing and shout the Jubilee !"

This is just a recap of some of the blessings God has showered on Jim and Hilda and our incredible family. Looking back, If Hilda and I hadn't become Christians, none of this would have happened.

CHAPTER EIGHT

I still haven't gotten over this incredible demonstration of God's abundant provision. In May 2006 I was driving down Interstate 5 on my way to Olympia, WA, to attend the National Day of Prayer to sing and to speak, when suddenly my 1987 Chrysler lost all power. I pulled off the road and asked the Lord to send someone to help me.

Then Sgt Robert Ritchie from Fort Lewis stopped and asked if he could help me. He used his cell phone to call my tow company, and waited with me until my car was towed away, and then drove me to Olympia. I had about an hour to share my faith with him. I told him that he wasn't there by chance but that God had brought him there to hear what I had to say about Jesus.

At the meeting, I just happened to be sitting next to a Major General who was the Chief Chaplain at Fort Lewis. I told him about my encounter with Sgt Ritchie, and he promised to contact him and follow up on my talk with him. The rotunda of the State Capitol was packed for the wonderful service, and the Chaplain's talk about the power of prayer was very inspiring. I spoke about "Why We Should Pray", and sang "Praise the Lord". After the service, friends drove me home.

Now here is where this story gets interesting. The next day the auto mechanic told my that my Chrysler wasn't worth fixing, it would cost too much, so I decided to let it go.

I wrote in my next *ACTION*GRAM that I had no money to buy another car, and if someone would like to donate a car to FACTS FOR FREEDOM I would be grateful. At our next FACTS rally Lauri Schiffman got up and made an appeal for someone to donate a car to FACTS.

After the meeting David Mason came up to me and said, "I would like to give you my car." Not even knowing what it was, I thanked him, and several days later Harold Jantz, a friend at church, drove me to David's house. When I saw the car David and his wife Marg gave me, I almost fell over. It was an Infiniti Q45, looking like it just came off the show room floor, with only 62,000 miles on it. When it was new it cost $65,000. They also had four brand-new tires installed. What a blessing !

There is no question in my mind what motivated this wonderful Christian couple to do this very generous act -- God works in mysterious ways His wonders to perform!

CHAPTER NINE

When I was a kid walking around in knickers, the world I lived in then was totally different than it is today. All the stores were closed on Sunday, and the nightclubs were shut down. The only way you could get drugs was to go the opium dens in Chinatown.

Do you remember in the movie "Gone With The Wind" when Rhett Butler said to Scarlett O'Hara at the end, "Frankly my dear, I don't give a damn" ? Our nation was in a state of shock that the film industry would allow profanity in a movie. Today, "Jesus Christ: and "God Damn" and even more profane and obscene words are an everyday part of our English language. It's difficult to turn on the TV or go to a movie or play and NOT hear the "f-word" and worse.

All the time I was growing up, until I joined the Coast Guard, if you wanted to look at a picture of a naked woman, you had to see it in the National Geographic magazine. Now you can see naked women by just turning on your TV, going to a movie, looking at a computer or going to an adult book store or porn shop, or for that matter almost any supermarket where there are dozens of magazines to choose from showing half-naked women and men, or you can even have porn delivered directly to your home or view it secretly on your computer, at home or at work, even school.

Today in the land of the free and the home of the brave, all the stores, strip clubs, porn shops and supermarkets where they all sell booze are wide open to kids, seven days and nights a week.

In other words our churches, Christian government and citizens have permitted all this to happen. This is supposed to be a government of the people, by the people and for the people. Yet some if the biggest destroyers are allowed to prosper, like the American Civil Liberties Union; (I call it "Anti-Christian Liberties Union"); People For the American Way; Hollywood; and the National Education Association, teaching our children from kindergarten and up that homosexuality is okay, even same-sex marriage -- SAY WHAT ??

These are some of the enemies of God, Christianity and the Bible; the abortion rights crowd, the homosexual army, the pornographers, the National Association of Women feminist crowd, drugs sold anywhere and everywhere, liberal politicians, and judges who cater to these people just to stay in power.

This is just the tip of the iceberg. America has been sold down the river by the men and women who sit on the Supreme Court, looking all dignified in their black robes, as they tear this country apart with their Supreme Court rulings. Do you remember in the 1960s when they used their authority to misinterpret the separation of church and state ?

This false interpretation has been promoted for so long over and over by liberal politicians, the media and the judges, and the American people have BOUGHT THE LIE.

Here are the facts and the truth that America's enemies ignore: THE BILL OF RIGHTS ARTICLE I: "CONGRESS SHALL MAKE no law respecting an establishment of religion." In other words they were forbidden to promote any government religion (That was the major reason people left England, because the King declared which religion the people must follow); prohibiting the free exercise thereof; or abridging the freedom of speech or of the press; of the right of the people peaceably to assemble; and to petition to government for a redress of grievances.

For FACTS FOR FREEDOM, I have researched the things that affect the Body of Christ, the family, and God's Church for 22 years. I am also a student of Biblical prophecy and it is my opinion that we are very close to the time for Jesus to fulfill the prophecies that predicted His return to earth.

Here are some of the indications of the breakdown of the human race and its destruction: The blessings of God and the abundant life He promised are not all fun and games. A major blessing He gave me is when He appointed me a watchman on the wall; Ezekiel 33: 6-7, "But if the watchman sees the enemy coming and doesn't sound the alarm and warn the people, he is responsible for their deaths. They will die in their sins, but I will charge the watchman for their deaths. So with you, son of man, I have appointed you as a watchman for the people."

My job as I see it is to warn God's people that the enemy is not only approaching but has saturated every facet of our courts, government, schools and culture. FACTS has sounded the alarm for 22 years. Sometimes I wonder if the pastors and Christians are listening.

Ezek. 33: 9, "But if you warn him to repent and he doesn't, he will die in sin and you will not be responsible."

When the Supreme Court in the 1960s banned prayer in school (separation of church and state), and when they banned the Ten Commandments from schools and government buildings (separation of church and state), the Supreme Court's written ruling was that they were afraid American children might read the Commandments and act on them, i.e. "Thou shalt not kill, thou shalt not steal, thou shalt not bear falsewitness against thy neighbor, thou shalt not kill, thou shalt not commit adultery, thou shalt not steal, thou shalt not covet."

Truly that is the most idiotic decision I have ever heard. They were AFRAID children would obey and not kill, not steal, not lie, etc. I can clearly see the hand of Satan. these decisions that affect us all are not only coming from the U.S. Supreme Court, but also the judges who legislate from the bench in the State Supreme Courts.

Please don't misinterpret me; not all judges are corrupt and evil. In fact there are many judges that are honestly doing the job they are supposed to do, and our hats are off to them. The problem as I see it is that the bad guys always seem to be winning. It is my opinion that terrorism, threats of wars, nuclear threats, venereal disease such as AIDS, easy divorce, etc. are all fitting a pattern of Biblical prophecy telling of the second coming of Jesus Christ.

Follow me as I lay out the way the U.S. Congress can stop judges from ruling on issues that they have no authorization for: marriage, abortion, homosexuality, what is taught in our schools, pornography, moral issues, the family, etc. Those are to be left up to the state governments, the state school boards and the American citizens.

The Constitution states in Article III Section 2, "In all the other cases before mentioned, the Supreme Court shall have appellate jurisdiction, both as to Law and Fact, with such exceptions under such regulations as the Congress shall make." There you have it ! The Constitutional Truth ! The American people must light a fire under their Congressmen and women and DEMAND action on the above issues. The Bible warns, Hosea 4:6, "My people perish for a lack of knowledge."

GET THE WORD OUT TO FAMILY AND FRIENDS.

CONCLUSION

I have been studying the Bible for 45 years and I believe it gives us the key and the answer why the U.S. and Canada have so many unsolvable problems. If you look at God's pattern with the Jews and apply that pattern to us today, you will see that the two fit together. Our nations are sick, our people are sick spiritually, physically and mentally; lost and frightened. Our leaders don't know which way to turn with the problems of terrorism, threats of nuclear wars, pornography, homosexuality and gay marriage, abortion, over 50% divorce rate, broken homes, immorality, crime, violence, racism, wanton vandalism and stealing like the world has never known before.

Our nations have put their trust in themselves and turned their backs on God and now are worshiping instead their idols of materialism, TV, booze, drugs, sex, power and greed. If you read Jeremiah and Isaiah, you will see how God used these men to warn the Jewish nation if they didn't turn from their evil ways God would destroy them. America and Canada are following the Jewish pattern. Our countries were built and established by men of God, praising Him and seeking His way. But since World War II bit by bit, we have become nations that have ignored God's way to live and prosper; I believe with all my heart that unless we heed this warning in Deut. 6: 12 and 8: 11-14, God will destroy our beautiful land. There is still hope, but only if we seek God's face through Jesus Christ.

This book is meant to show God's hand at work when a man and his wife and family turn their backs on the world, the flesh and the devil, and follow Jesus instead. Knowing what is going on in the world and that life is so uncertain is the reason Hilda and

I always stressed the importance of being assured of where we all will spend eternity: Heaven, not hell.

As we look at the deplorable condition of our government and culture let us not forget that we who claim Jesus Christ as Lord and Savior need not worry or be afraid. Are you sure where your eternal home will be ? I AM !!!

WE WIN !!

IN JESUS' NAME AND FOR HIS GLORY,

James C. Galbraith

A FINAL WORD
or two:

This book could not have been finished without the incredible
talented Alice Jackson working with me for over a year.
Alice is also an author who has had several articles published.
She is my best friend, a gift from God.

~ JIM ~

*   *   *   *   *   *   *   *   *

[Jim is an extraordinary man
whose strong spiritual strength has led him
through many difficult steps throughout his Christian life.
From his first few (as I thought!) pages and
handwritten notes for his book,
detail after detail emerged from his marvelous memory.
Working with him on this book has been a gift from the Lord .
He is my best friend, in complete faith and trust.]

~ alice ~

PHOTOGRAPHS

Church in Boston where Jim & Hilda were married

Jim "Popeye the Sailor Man"

Jim's & Hilda's wedding reception
L to R: Bob, Fran, Jim, Hilda and her brother
Bill

Jim with his mom at Leon & Eddie's
nightclub in New York City, WWII

Hilda's sister Fran and her
three boyfriends

Hilda's commanding officer (center)
and her staff. Hilda is second from the
right

Jim's shipmates from PF-17, the
USS Key West, during WWII

Jim and his brother Bob

Air France magazine ad

Mamie van Doren, Aqua Velva
commercial

Magazine ad for Kodak
Cameras

Jim, when he was working on TV
commercials

Jim's great-grandfather's
outhouse at the old farm

Hilda cutting grass at the farm

Our picnic grove at the farm

Jim, a true Scot, Campbell
Clan

Jim at NJ farm with "Halleluja"

Hilda and Helen at the Arc d' Triomphe,
Paris

Daughter Helen, talking to
Dad (in French policeman's
uniform)

Hilda, Helen & Jim's Mom at a German
Gun Bunker of World War II, Normandy
Coast, France

Galbraith Stores Chain, all over Scotland

Hlda & Helen at the
London Bridge

Jim Speaking at Amway Rally

Hilda showing Amway marketing plan

Jim teaching at his Amway office

Hilda speaking at Amway convention

Galbraith weekend Amway Convention
L to R: Dick & Dee Ossinger, Jim, Hilda
& Skip Ross

Amway Rally at Galbraith Cottage, On "Queen Mary"
Pontoon Boat & Dock

Galbraith Amway Leaders at Rally on Peter Island in
the Bahamas

Hilda's brothers & sisters. Top L to R: Clark, Brennice, Hilda, Peggy & Fran

Jim marching his grandchildren down the road for a walk in the woods

Jima playing "Who's Got the Nickel" with his grandchildren

Jim's granddaughters Jessica & Juliana ...

... watching their sister Emily dancing with their Dad (Keith)

Jim, Hilda, & their three great-
grandchildren

David & Jessica Gray
Forest & Lauren Sky

Emily & Bryson Wegner with Kellen

All of Jim & Hilda's
grandchildren & great-
grandchildren

The Troutt family, Jeffrey & Helen, Rebecca, Hilda, Jim in back, Brittney & Ashley

Kellen watching "Pop-Pop" on TV show, 700 Club

Jessica in Jim's sailor uniform

Jessica in Hilda's uniform

Jim singing "Wind Beneath My Wings" at his & Hilda's 50th Wedding anniversary

Jim singing "Praise the Lord" on
the 700 Club TV show

Jim in costume to read the first
prayer that was ever prayed in the
U.S. Congress, Washington D.C.

TV Commercial for "Galbraith for
Congress"

Jim after running for
Congress in 1984

Jim & Hilda with Pastor Scott
Montagne

Jim, fishing on Pastor Rose's boat
with Jeffrey Troutt & friends in
Alaska

Jim with a 22 pound Silver
Salmon in Alaska

Please buy my book!

Pastor Chuck Murray who led Jim, Hilda &
son James to Jesus Christ, and to Amway

ABOUT THE AUTHOR

Jim Galbraith has had an active busy life with his family, mostly centered around his strong Christian faith in the Lord, our Savior Jesus Christ and the Holy Spirit.   He has been a well-known TV commercial actor; a business leader for Amway Products; a Christian conservative political leader; plus his ministry in the Bread of Life, homeless men's mission. At age 81, and recovering from knee joint replacement surgery, he does all his own work at home, from cooking and housecleaning to tending his garden and yard, looking after his two dogs and four horses. He lives in the Puyallup, Washington area, near his son and grandchildren, and regularly visits his daughter and her family in Alaska where he is a true enthusiastic and avid fisherman. Jim has many friends throughout the U.S.

Printed in the United States
136426LV00003B/7/P